To Patricia Muldoon for the gift
of her friendship, Jorge

To Marietjie and Catherina
with love, Piet

A Patricia Muldoon por el regalo
de su amistad, Jorge

Para Marietjie y Catherina
con amor, Piet

Text copyright © 2006 by Jorge Luján
Illustrations copyright © 2006 by Piet Grobler
English translation copyright © 2007 by Elisa Amado
First published in Spanish as *Accidente celeste* by Fondo de Cultura
Económica in 2006
First bilingual edition published in Canada and the USA by Groundwood
Books in 2007
11 10 09 08 07   1 2 3 4 5

Groundwood Books / House of Anansi Press
110 Spadina Avenue, Suite 801, Toronto, ON, Canada M5V 2K4
Distributed in the USA by Publishers Group West
1700 Fourth Street, Berkeley, CA 94710

We acknowledge for their financial support of our publishing
program the Canada Council for the Arts, the Government of Canada
through the Book Publishing Industry Development Program (BPIDP) and
the Ontario Arts Council.

Library and Archives Canada Cataloging in Publication
Luján, Jorge
Sky blue accident / Jorge Luján; illustrations by Piet Grobler; translated by
Elisa Amado = Accidente celeste / Jorge Luján;
ilustraciones de Piet Grobler; traducción de Elisa Amado
Text in English and Spanish.
ISBN-13: 978-0-88899-805-7
ISBN-10: 0-88899-805-8
1. Picture books for children. I. Grobler, Piet II. Amado, Elisa
III. Title. IV. Title: Accidente celeste.
PZ73.L85Sk 2007   j861   C2006-904739-1

The illustrations are in gouache and pastel.
Printed and bound in China

Texto © 2006 de Jorge Luján
Ilustración © 2006 de Piet Grobler
Traducción © 2007 de Elisa Amado
Este libro fue publicado originalmente en español por Fondo
de Cultura Económica en el 2006
Primera edición bilingüe publicada en Canadá y en los
Estados Unidos por Groundwood Books en el 2007
11 10 09 08 07   1 2 3 4 5

Groundwood Books / House of Anansi Press
110 Spadina Avenue, Suite 801, Toronto, ON, Canada M5V 2K4
Distribuido en los Estados Unidos por Publishers Group West
1700 Fourth Street, Berkeley, CA 94710

Agradecemos el apoyo financiero otorgado a nuestro programa de
publicaciones por el Canada Council for the Arts, el gobierno de Canadá
por medio del Book Publishing Industry Development Program (BPIDP) y
el Ontario Arts Council.

Library and Archives Canada Cataloging in Publication
Luján, Jorge
Sky blue accident / Jorge Luján; illustrations by Piet Grobler; translated by
Elisa Amado = Accidente celeste / Jorge Luján; ilustraciones de Piet
Grobler; traducción de Elisa Amado
Text in English and Spanish.
ISBN-13: 978-0-88899-805-7
ISBN-10: 0-88899-805-8
1. Picture books for children. I. Grobler, Piet II. Amado, Elisa
III. Title. IV. Title: Accidente celeste.
PZ73.L85Sk 2007   j861   C2006-904739-1

Las ilustraciones fueron realizadas en aguazo y pastel.
Impreso y encuadernado en China

40 YEARS · 40 ANS
ONTARIO ARTS COUNCIL
CONSEIL DES ARTS DE L'ONTARIO

Sky Blue Accident

Accidente celeste

Jorge Luján

illustrations by * ilustraciones de
Piet Grobler

translated by * traducción Elisa Amado

Groundwood Books * Libros Tigrillo

HOUSE OF ANANSI PRESS   TORONTO   BERKELEY

Once on a misty morning
I crashed into the sky,

Una mañana de brumas
me tropecé con el cielo

then hid its broken pieces
in my pocket.

y a los pedazos caídos
los escondí en mi bolsillo.

"Hey, do you want to see these, teacher?" I said, holding out my hand.

¿Quiere mirarlos, maestra?, dije estirando la mano,

She grew wings on her back
and flew out the window.

y a ella le crecieron alas
y escapó por la ventana.

Lost clouds stumbled around
bumbling into corners,

Las nubes andan perdidas
chocándose en las esquinas.

while the moon directed traffic
through empty spaces.

la luna dirige el tráfico
mas lo que sobra es espacio.

Then the children ran up
and began to paint a new sky.

Los chicos llegan corriendo
y pintan un cielo nuevo,

But they were missing a piece,
so I gave them...

les falta un trozo y les doy...

bits of the real one.

añicos del verdadero.